Dear Parent:

Your child's love of reading starts here!

Every child learns to read in a different way and at his or her own speed. You can help your young reader improve and become more confident by encouraging his or her own interests and abilities. You can also guide your child's spiritual development by reading stories with biblical values and Bible stories, like I Can Read! books published by Zonderkidz. From books your child reads with you to the first books he or she reads alone, there are I Can Read! books for every stage of reading:

SHARED READING
Basic language, word repetition, and whimsical illustrations, ideal for sharing with your emergent reader.

BEGINNING READING
Short sentences, familiar words, and simple concepts for children eager to read on their own.

READING WITH HELP
Engaging stories, longer sentences, and language play for developing readers.

READING ALONE
Complex plots, challenging vocabulary, and high-interest topics for the independent reader.

ADVANCED READING
Short paragraphs, chapters, and exciting themes for the perfect bridge to chapter books.

I Can Read! books have introduced children to the joy of reading since 1957. Featuring award-winning authors and illustrators and a fabulous cast of beloved characters, I Can Read! books set the standard for beginning readers.

A lifetime of discovery begins with the magical words **"I Can Read!"**

Visit www.icanread.com for information on enriching your child's reading experience.
Visit www.zonderkidz.com for more Zonderkidz I Can Read! titles.

This is the day the LORD has made;
let us rejoice and be glad in it.
—Psalm 118:24

To Bella, who loves to play.
—S.H.

ZONDERKIDZ

Howie Wants to Play

Requests for information should be addressed to:
Zonderkidz, 3900 *Sparks Drive SE, Grand Rapids, Michigan 49546*

Library of Congress Cataloging-in-Publication Data

Henderson, Sara, 1952-
Howie wants to play / story by Sara Henderson ; pictures by Aaron Zenz.
p. cm. — (I can read! My first level)
Summary: Howie gets into all kinds of mischief while Emma chases and finally catches him, reassures him that God loves him even when he makes a mess, and shows him that playing is what puppies do best.
ISBN 978-0-310-71604-4 (softcover)
[1. Dogs—Fiction. 2. Animals—Infancy—Fiction. 3. Christian life—Fiction.] I. Zenz, Aaron, ill. II. Title.
PZ7.H3835Hoy 2008
[E]—dc22 2007034316

Art Direction: Jody Langley
Cover Design: Sarah Molegraaf

Printed in the United States of America

17 18 19 20 21 LSCC 10 9 8 7 6 5 4 3

I Can Read!™

Howie Wants to Play

story by Sara Henderson

pictures by Aaron Zenz

Good morning, Howie!

It’s time to get up.

It’s time to play.

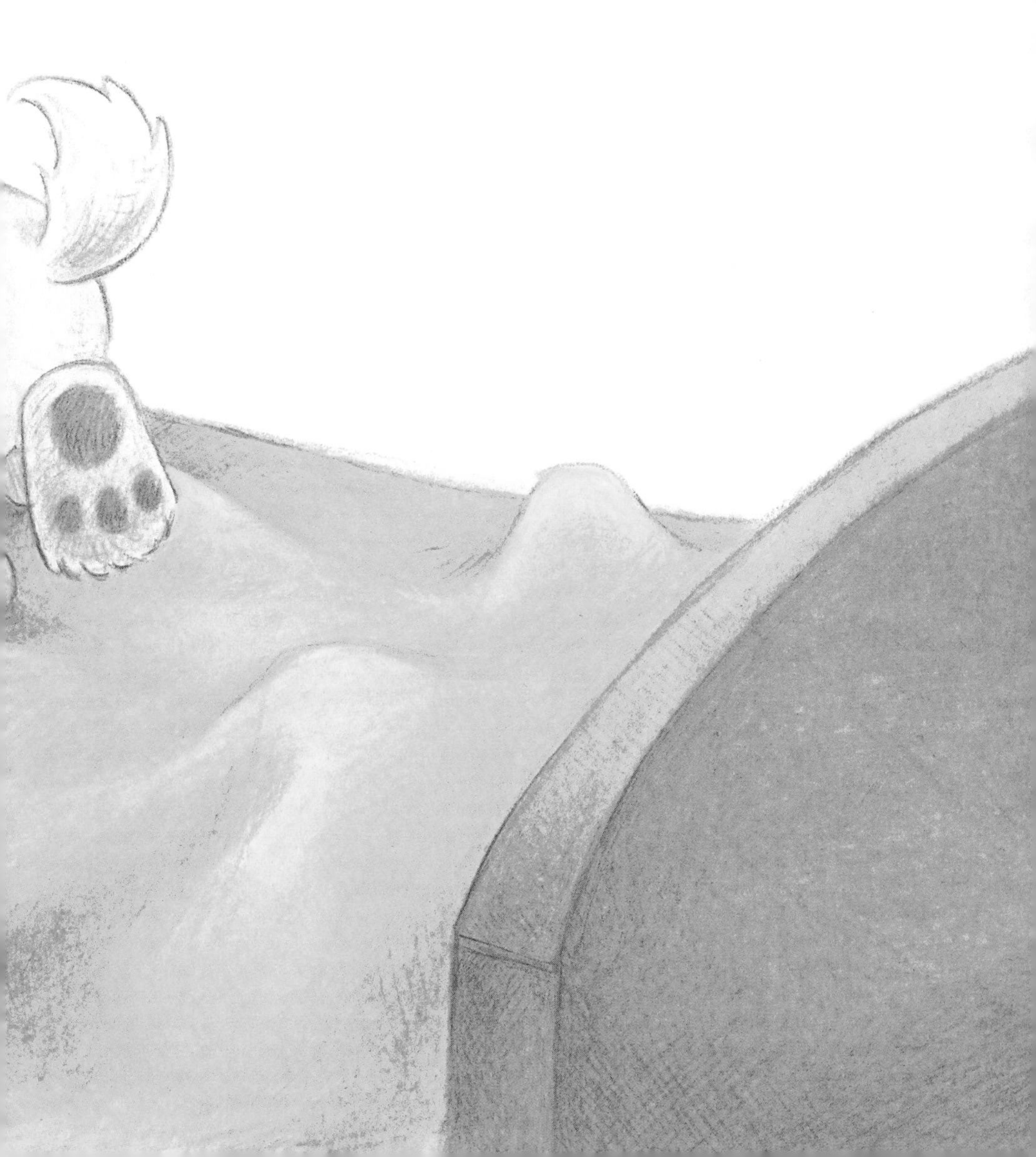

Wait, Howie, wait!
I have to get dressed.

Where did Howie go?

Clang, bang,

clatter, crash,

rattle, rattle,

BOOM!

Uh-oh!

Howie's in the kitchen.

“Out, Howie, out!”
said Sister.

"What a terrible mess!
Puppies can't eat cereal.
Emma, get your puppy!"

But where did Howie go?

Clang, bang,

clatter, crash,

rattle, rattle,

BOOM!

Uh-oh!

Howie's in the family room.

"Out, Howie, out!"
said Brother.

“What a terrible mess!
Puppies can’t play blocks.
Emma, get your puppy!”

But where did Howie go?
Clang, bang,

clatter, crash,

rattle, rattle,

BOOM!

Uh-oh!

Howie's at the front door.

“Out, Howie, out!” said Dad.

“What a terrible mess!
Puppies can’t go to work.
Emma, get your puppy!”

But where did Howie go?

Clang, bang,

clatter, crash,

rattle, rattle,

BOOM!

Uh-oh!

Howie's in the garden.

"Out, Howie, out!" said Mom.

"What a terrible mess!
Puppies can't plant flowers.
Emma, get your puppy!"

But where did Howie go?

Oh no!

Stop, Howie, stop!
Your paws are all muddy.
You'll make a terrible mess.

Howie, you are little
just like me.

I know you didn't mean
to make a mess.

I'll clean you up, Howie.

We won’t make
any more messes today.

Did you know God loves us even when we make messes?

That's what my daddy says.

Come, Howie, come.

Let's do what puppies do best.

Let's play!